The Guiding Pen

Brittany Benko

Published by Brittany Benko, 2024.

THE GUIDING PEN

First edition. March 29, 2024.

Copyright © 2024 Brittany Benko.

ISBN: 979-8224826063

Written by Brittany Benko.

Table of Contents

This collection is dedicated to my beautiful daughter, Nicole. I hope these words help and guide you on your journey through life.

Mother's Guidance

With gentle words, a mother lends her ear.
To tales of joy and whispered fear
Her wisdom, like a gentle breeze,
Navigates love's stormy seas.
Through laughter's dance and tears that fall,
She shares the secrets of love's call.
A beacon shining in the night,
Her love, a steadfast, guiding light.
As seasons pass and hearts entwine,
She teaches strength and love's design.
To cherish self and know her worth,
In love's embrace, to find her mirth.
Through years that pass, her daughter grows.
With every challenge, love bestows.
A mother's guidance, deeply sown,
In love's journey, she's not alone.

A Mother's Love

From the first breath, a connection divine,
A mother's love, an eternal lifeline.
With tender arms, she cradles her child.
Whispering lullabies, dreams beguiled.
Through moonlit night and dawning days,
She showers affection in countless ways.
In each triumph and every defeat, she stands by her daughter.
A love complete.
With words of wisdom, she paints life's art.
Nurturing dreams while igniting a spark.
She sees her reflection in those innocent eyes.
A world of possibilities, and endless sky.
Through laughter and tears, joys and strife,
A mother's love becomes the thread of life.
It's a symphony of grace, a melody strong.
Guiding her daughter, where she belongs.
She weaves dreams into reality's seam,
Believing in her daughter's limitless dream.
As time moves on, and years slip away,
The bond grows stronger is what people say.
For a mother's love, like a timeless river,
Flows eternal, an unbroken quiver.
So, let us honor this love divine.
A mother's love, a treasure so fine.
For in her heart a daughter will see,
The purest love until eternity.

All I Want

All I want, my girl, is for you to be happy.
I want to see you smiling each day.
With that flush of warmth on your cheeks that causes you to glow.
I want you to soar high in the sky like an eagle.
Fearless, carefree, and magnificent.
I want to know your heart will be full with each choice you make in life.
The journey you are on should be cherished, not full of heartache.
All I want for you is joy.
However you can obtain delight.
Grab onto that and never lose your grasp.
Take chances and go after what you want, even if you don't obtain your
goal in the end.
Life is too short to be anything but happy.

An Ever-Changing Journey

My sweet girl, life is an ever-changing journey.
Change can be both exciting and daunting.
It's something we all must navigate while moving forward through life.
Remember that change is a natural part of life.
Just as the seasons change and the world around us evolves,
so, too, will our own lives.
Embrace change as an opportunity of growth, even when it feels
uncomfortable.
Change leads to personal development and discovering new aspects of
ourselves.

Baby Girl

Baby girl, cast your troubles to the Lord.
Do not panic while feeling ignored.
Baby girl, do not be stressed.
By the end of the day, know that you've done your best.
Baby girl, pray for strength.
God will guide you through tough times.
Baby girl, you are not alone.
Believe in this knowledge when you are grown.

Balance

Guard your heart with your mind,
And guide your mind with your heart.
There has to be a balance in order to live a wonderful life.

Be Kind

Dearest daughter, remember to always be kind.
Even if hate begins to rise in your chest.
There will be times when you may yearn to get even with those who
wronged you.
I myself have wasted energy on people who will never change,
And I wish I could go back in time and grant myself peace by walking
away.
Being kind is not always the easiest route,
But showing kindness will make you feel better in the end.
Anger takes away your happiness.
Don't let the world bring out your worst.
Remember to always be kind for your well being.

Be Patient

Be patient, my daughter.
Even a rainbow will not appear in the sky until after a rainfall.
Sometimes, not even then.
But, your time will come.

Beautiful Girl

Beautiful girl, do not succumb to peer pressure.
You are uniquely and beautifully made.
Beautiful girl, do not be afraid to chase your dreams.
Life is full of risks, so take chances on opportunities that speak to your
heart.
Beautiful girl, you are strong and capable of doing what you want in life.
Be the girl who goes after what she wants.
Remember there are many roads to the path you choose.
Life is a journey, so make your moments memorable.

Bloom

When you evolve,
Don't announce it to the world.
Just bloom.

Blossoming

S weet girl,
You will bloom with radiance regardless if you are wanted by others.

The key to blossoming is to water your own garden.

Chin Up

If people knock you off your way,
Hold your chin up anyway.
Humans are cruel and sometimes mean.
They like to act out and create a scene.
When a person is down, their actions become grim.
While they seek attention, stay silent and swim.
You'll run into people who have pure hearts.
This is where life truly starts.
Life is about the people you meet.
True souls are what makes a life complete.

Daughter

D is for the delight you bring each day
A beacon of light in every way
Uplifting spirits with your warm embrace
Gently filling hearts with love and grace
Holding dreams like stars up in the sky
Tenderly watching them soar up high
Eternal bond between us remains
Rising above life's trials and pains

Daughter of Mine

You're growing up, daughter of mine
You may be scared, but you'll do fine
Daughter of mine, I see you
Pushing yourself through and through
Daughter of mine, take deep breaths
Life will always seem complex
Daughter of mine, prepare for change
Chapters in life must be rearranged
Daughter of mine, plan ahead
Educate yourself and be well read
Daughter of mine, be composed
Do your best not to become exposed
Daughter of mine, I'll hold your hand
You'll make mistakes, but you'll never be banned
Daughter of mine, you'll always be loved
I promise you that with the flow of my blood

Dear Daughter

I may not be your coolest friend,
But I'll stick by you until the end
Your demeanor is strong and your heart is kind
You can do anything within due time
Your fire within glows like a light
Shining bright like a star at night
Do not follow trends
Be a leader instead
Think with your heart as well has your head
When in doubt, look above
The answers you seek will be shown with love

Don't Be Afraid

My darling girl,
Don't be afraid of the future.
Not knowing where you are headed is a part of life's exciting journey.
My love,
Don't be afraid of being imperfect.
There will be so much pressure to be the best at everything.
Please remember that people have different strengths and weaknesses.
Focus on what you can master.
Don't beat yourself up when you are not like others.
Don't be afraid of ending up somewhere other than where you envisioned.
There are many destinations where we can end up,
And each destination provides different aspects of happiness.

Don't Stress

Remember that nothing is set in stone. Don't stress about a bad situation. It is sure to change.

Don't Waste Years

Think of the person you can turn out to be if you don't waste years trying to be someone else.

Each Path

I'd like for you to think things through
Some decisions require thought
There are paths you alone decide to pursue
Each path has a lesson to be taught
When you go about your day,
Consider all of your options
Take the time to meditate and pray
Hearing your inner voice helps you to be confident in your steps
Think of what you want in life
Time does not stop while you choose
Be picky when you become a wife
Make sure your partner has all the same views
I hope I've helped you on the way to becoming a woman in this life
It's been a pleasure raising you
I hope you get where you need to be

Embrace Your Authenticity

In the depths of your soul, lies a spark divine
A journey to embrace, a truth to find
Shredding pretense, you'll come alive
Becoming your authentic self, you'll thrive
Unfurl the petals of your hidden dreams
In authenticity, your spirit redeems
Embrace the flaws, for they make you whole
Unveil the essence that lies in your soul
Like a butterfly, break free from the cocoon
You'll soar to heights, beneath the moon
With each step you take, your heart will dance
In rhythm of truth, you'll find your trance
Fear not the judgment, let doubts depart
For in authenticity, you'll find your heart
Reveal your colors, shine without disguise
A masterpiece of truth before our eyes
So dare to be you, and let your light shine
In becoming your true self, life will align
For in this realm of existence, you play a part
Embrace your authenticity, let it guide your heart

Encourage the Light

There once was a mother so wise
Whose daughter had stars in her eyes
With love in her voice, she'd offer her choice
"Go, darling. Reach for the skies!"
Her words were like wings to take flight
Guiding her through challenges while shining bright
She'd whisper, "Believe, you'll surely achieve.
Your dreams are within your own sight."
Through hurdles and doubts that would loom,
Her mother would banish the gloom
With courage instilled, her daughter fulfilled,
Every goal, every hope would bloom
So let this tale serve as a guide
For mothers and daughters worldwide
With love as you might, encourage the light,
And watch as dreams beautifully glide

Encouragement

Embrace life with courage, my dear
Never let fear cloud your way
Courageous hearts, I want you to steer
Over mountains high, in skies so gray
United we stand, a bond so clear
Radiating love, come what may
And when you stumble, do not fear
Generations of strength pave your way
Encouragement flows, always near
Molding you, my daughter, day by day
Enable your authentic self
Never doubt who you are
Trust in yourself and you'll travel far

Faith in Yourself

My precious girl,

Throughout your life, you will face numerous challenges and obstacles. There will be moments when you doubt your abilities and question your worth. In those times, my darling, I want you to remember this: you have within you an immense wellspring of potential, strength, and resilience. You are capable of achieving anything you set your mind to.

Having faith in yourself doesn't mean you will never experience self-doubt. It means that even when those doubts arise, you will trust in your abilities and believe in your capacity to overcome adversity. It's about recognizing that you are your own greatest advocate and supporter.

Believing in yourself is like having a guiding light that leads you through the darkest of storms. It's about embracing your unique qualities, your dreams, and your aspirations.

Remember that making mistakes and facing failures are a part of the journey to success. Your faith in yourself will enable you to persevere through challenging times and emerge stronger and wiser.

Life will be unpredictable. There will be moments when your faith is tested. During these times, turn to the values, beliefs, and principles that define you. This will be your greatest ally on the journey called life.

Embrace your uniqueness, follow your dreams, and never forget to have faith in yourself.

False Promises

Actions speak louder than words.
Be sure to recognize fake people and false promises.

Floating

My beautiful girl,
Do not be afraid of the ocean.
Let the waves carry you where you need to be.
There's no need to fight where life will take you.
Be content with floating to another part of the shore.
Let your anxieties release as the sun caresses your face.
Let the water carry you to an unplanned destination.
It doesn't matter how you reach your destination.
Just be sure you enjoy the ride to your happy ending.

Glowing Heart

Your glowing heart I can't deny
Warm and vibrant with your spirit held high
Your glowing heart many admire
Gaining strength, your persistence is like fire
Your glowing heart intimidates many
You are as rare as a 1943 penny
Your glowing heart gives others light
Helping people stand upright

Home

Home is not a physical address.
It's a place where you surround yourself with your loved ones.
Home is family.

I Hope You Know

I hope you know how special you are
I know all mothers say this, but you are one in a million.
I hope you know there's nothing I wouldn't do for you.
If I had to experience unending pain in order for you to feel safe,
I'd endure pain one thousand times over.
I hope you know this chapter isn't your last.
You may be experiencing rain storms,
but the next chapter will radiate a colorful rainbow.
I hope you know how blessed I am that God put you in my life.
Children give life meaning,
and you've made every moment count.
I hope you know I'll never regret being your mother.
Some people find their soul mates through romantic partners.
Some even find them through a friend.
Through you, my daughter, my soul mate, I have found.

I Know a Girl

I know a girl
That girl is you
She always sees everything through
I know a girl who is the night
Like the moon,
She goes through phases while shining bright
I know a girl
She came from me
Her spirit is laid back and free
I know a girl
I call her mine
Like an angel in heaven,
She is divine

I See You

I see you trying not to fall
      While hanging out with friends
I see your tears and hear your call
I'll have your back until the very end
I see you trying to put on a show
Masking your true self
Trying to dig yourself out of snow,
You stay in a climate that's bitter cold
Know that there are people who bring out the golden sun
These people may not be who you desire,
But they are a breath of fresh air on a muggy day
Be sure to accept your inner self
Don't lie your charms upon a shelf

I'd Still Choose You

Through all the tears and all the pain,
I'd still choose you.
I'll never be irritated or complain that you're my loving daughter.
I may seem tired and fatigued.
Sometimes I'm overwhelmed.
Know that I'm extremely pleased even if sometimes I yell.
I'd still choose you everyday now until the end.
You're a part of me that makes me whole.
My sidekick and best friend.

I'll Guide You

I'll guide you, sweet girl
Through heartache and pain
When the going gets tough,
My love for you still remains
I'll guide you, sweet girl
When you become unsure
Be full of confidence while staying pure
I'll guide you, sweet girl
Wherever that will be
Even if we do not always seem to agree
I'll guide you, sweet girl
With all of my heart and soul
Your life is precious
Your happiness makes me whole

Kindness

Kindness, my sweet one, is a gift that has the power to illuminate the darkest corners of the world. It's a reminder that, no matter what challenges we face, there is always room for compassion and understanding.

I have seen you extend your hand to those in need, offer a warm smile to a stranger, and speak words of comfort to a friend going through a difficult time. Your kindness isn't just a collection of gestures; it's a reflection of genuine goodness within your heart.

Remember that kindness is not a weakness but a strength. It takes courage to be kind in a world that sometimes values toughness over tenderness. As you navigate through life, I encourage you to hold onto this precious quality and let it guide your actions.

In moments of doubt and uncertainty, let kindness be your compass. It will lead you towards understanding, forgiveness, and love. Kindness has the power to heal wounds and touch lives.

Always be the kind and compassionate soul that you are, for the world needs more people like you — individuals who can make a positive difference with a simple act of kindness. Your ability to bring warmth to the lives of others is a gift that I hope you continue to give generously.

Let Your Tears Fall

When you're in pain, I want to tell you everything will be okay.
I want to whisper hopeful promises that your journey will get better.
The truth is, sometimes life is messy and complicated.
Whenever you feel heartbroken, let your tears fall.
Do not be afraid to feel that hole in your chest.
You must let yourself feel that pain in order to move on.
That's how we let go of trauma.
Process what happened, then throw that unwanted emotion away.

Life's Truest Gifts

Do not be troubled from what you see
Release your anxieties and let your heart be free
Learn to accept what others cannot
Life does not bring happiness from materials bought
Remember to love yourself, family, and friends
They are life's truest gifts when we reach our end
I may not know the path you'll walk
Just know I support you and I'm your rock

Look to Your Heart

Whatever you choose in this life, know that I support you
Do not be fearful of what I may think
Embrace who you are, but respect that I may not agree with your
decisions
Figuring out who you are can take you down rocky roads
If you get lost, look to your heart
It holds all the answers if you are willing to listen

Love

Love, my sweet girl, is a mosaic of emotions. It's a fragile dance, a journey of self-discovery, and a fabric woven with threads of vulnerability.

Love, my darling, is like a gentle rain that falls when you least expect it. It's in the way your heart skips a beat when you see someone, the way your laughter harmonizes with their own. It's in the way your soul recognizes each other, as if they have met in another lifetime.

Love, dear, often comes with tears. But, remember, those tears nourish the roots of your resilience. They're the rain that helps you grow, the pain that makes you stronger. Love's flow is what sculpts your character.

Mistakes are stepping stones to understanding, love's gentle tutors. Each misstep brings you closer to the love that is genuine, the one that will stand the test of time. You learn from the wrong choices and mold them into the right ones.

Remember, in love, you'll find a reflection of your own beauty, an affirmation of your worth. It's a journey that unfolds over time. Like chapters of a book that you'll write together. Embrace it, cherish it, and know that I'll always be here to guide you through its ever-changing pages.

Moments

Nobody's lives are perfect.
Each of us will experience sadness, joy, and pain.
There will be perfect days and moments when you feel like giving up.
I will always wish your sorrows away, but we all have to experience the
lows in order to appreciate the happy moments in life.

My Cherished Daughter

From the moment you entered this world,
My precious gem, my darling girl,
I vowed to be your guiding light
To walk beside you, day and night
Through stormy seas and turbulent tides,
I'll steer you to shores where love abides
When doubts arise and fears take hold,
I'll be the anchor, steadfast and bold
With gentle words, I'll calm your soul
And nurture dreams that make you whole
Embrace your worth, my darling daughter
With courage, grace, and endless water
Let your voice soar, unbridled and free
For within you lies pure majesty
Seek truth and kindness, side by side
Let empathy be your steadfast guide
Embrace diversity, let judgements cease
In unity, find harmony and inner peace
Remember, my love, you're never alone
Though time may pass, our hearts are sown
So, my dear, as you spread your wings
Unveiling the world that adventure bring
Know that my love will never falter
Guiding you, my cherished daughter

My Daughter

You've grown into a woman, brave and true
For all that you are, my thanks I bestow
In your eyes, I glimpse the world anew
A reflection of the love I've poured into you
From the depths of my soul, I express my delight
For you, my daughter, bring eternal light
You've gifted me moments, both big and small
And taught me lessons, profound and tall
For every sacrifice, you've repaired with care
A bond between us, unbreakable and rare
Through laughter and tears, we've shared a dance
A symphony of love, in every circumstance
My gratitude, a river that will never cease
For you, my daughter, bring my heart peace

My Hope for You

My hope for you is that you experience life to the fullest while also staying safe.

Step on stones that give you pure joy, and avoid the stones that look like they'll topple over.

My hope for you is you'll be a sunflower in a garden full of roses.

Roses may be admired, but a sunflower stands tall with a sunny demeanor.

My hope for you is that you'll treat others and yourself with kindness.

This world needs more compassionate people, so sprinkle love wherever you can.

My hope for you is that you find meaning in life.

Your journey will not always be effortless, so find comfort in something that will satisfy your soul.

My hope for you is that you look into the mirror and become friends with the woman you see.

She will be your biggest ally, the reason you keep pushing forward, and, sometimes, your only friend.

My hope for you is that you feel comfortable in your own skin.

The media will brainwash you into thinking you need to look a certain way, but real beauty comes from embracing your natural features.

My hope for you is that you can pave your own path to your desired destination.

It's good not to follow your friend's every step in life.

Just be sure the end of the road is where you want to be.

My hope for you is that you hold this guidance close to your heart.

Always know I am with you during your rain storms.

I have confidence you will find a rainbow when the sun reappears.

My Medicine

My girl,
I love taking care of you.
It healed the wounded part of me when I needed someone to take care
of myself.
You are my medicine.

My Sun and Stars

You may not know this, but you are my sun and stars.
Your smile is like the sun that warms my soul.
Heat waves of adoration fill my veins when I speak of you.
Your presence shines like a star in the sky.
Keep that light within you.
Stand out like the sun, stars, and the moon.
Attract the eyes of many with an innocent demeanor.
Try to be an example to young girls.
They are always looking for someone to follow.
Become the light from the sun and stars you were meant to be.

Never Settle

Young girl,
Never settle for less than what you want.
There's a world of possibilities to be discovered.
Just be sure to walk through a door that will lead you to the next one.

Nurturing Dreams

In a world where the teenage years roam,
A mother's love finds its true home
With guidance so keen,
She's a steady routine
Nurturing dreams as they're sown

Patching Wounded Holes

My days were empty before you arrived
I was depressed and barely survived
You poured out sunlight into my soul
Patching up my wounded holes
You rescued me from my solitude
Like a white knight chasing away monsters,
You helped me fight
This damsel fell in love with you
Making my dream of being a mother come true

Peace to Your Soul

My child,
Stay close to the people who give peace to your soul. This will help you stay refreshed and content.

Pebbles in the Sand

We are all pebbles in the sand
Waiting to do our parts
Let's help each other by walking hand in hand
We have the potential to become lovely works of art
You are the pebble in the sand
Waiting to float out to sea
Waiting for an adventure
Your soul longs to be free
We may be pebbles in the sand that are often overlooked
Each pebble has a purpose
Stay true to the story in your book

Perfect in my Eyes

You're perfect in my eyes, you see
Beautiful and wild as the sparkling sea
I'll never erase your lovely flaws
They make you who you are
Never let a man tell you otherwise
You'll end up with wounded scars
Hold your head high and be confident in your true self
The world needs your presence
Place yourself high upon that shelf

Proud of You

As I look at the young lady you've become, I am filled with awe and admiration for the person you are turning into. You are growing up into a remarkable young woman, and I want you to know how proud I am of you. Your journey through your teenage years has not been without challenges, and yet, you have faced them with grace, strength, and resilience. Your ability to adapt, learn, and grow from your experiences is truly remarkable.

I am proud of your unwavering commitment to your education, your dedication to passions, and your desire to pursue your dreams. Your curiosity and thirst for knowledge are qualities that will serve you well throughout your life.

What I'm most proud of, my dearest, is your unwavering sense of self. You have not allowed the pressure and expectations of the world to define you. You've been true to your values, and you continue to stand tall with your head held high, always striving to make the right choices, even when it's not the easiest path.

Your journey into adulthood can be challenging, and there will be times when you face difficult decisions and moments of self-doubt. Please know I have the utmost faith in you. Your courage, wisdom, and intuition will guide you through those times, just as they have brought you this far.

Always remember that you have a strong, supportive, loving family. I am here for you, cheering you along the way. Embrace every moment, continue to be true to yourself, and never stop chasing your dreams. The world is a better place with you in it, and I am so grateful to be your mother.

Recharge

Dearest daughter,
Be sure to take time to relax after indulging in the business of your day.
There will always be tasks that need to be done.
Be sure you plug in your own batteries so you can recharge for the next
day.

Sparkling Soul

My sweet child,
Never forget your worth.
You are comparable to a diamond,
Blinding everyone with your sparkling soul.

Storms

Remember that storms are a natural part of life.
    If you can endure them,
There will be a vibrant rainbow to view towards its end.

Sunbeam

You create warmth like a sunbeam during the darkest night
Providing positivity with all of your might
Others see your candle burning
I hope you see it too
Remember how far you've come when you're feeling blue

The Lady

I'm proud of the lady you're growing into
Sticking to your beliefs like glue
Your gentle soul and sharp mind
Helps you climb the mountains you find
You do not crumble when things go south
You're careful and keen when choosing your route
The advice I'll give is humble and true
Keep my words in mind when you know not what to do

The Phoenix Flies

Be true to yourself, in all you do
Authenticity shall see you through
Let not the world dictate your worth
You're a masterpiece since your day of birth
Seek knowledge, for it is a flame
That burns eternal, fuels your aim
The power of learning, never subside
It ignites your spirit, opens wide
Remember, darling, to wear grace
In every step, in every space
Kindness is an ointment, a soothing touch
It mends hearts and heals so much
In love, my dear, find your solace
But guard your heart, be wise, embrace
Have faith in yourself, don't lose the way
Within your soul, a guiding ray
Cherish moments, fleeting and bright
In laughter's embrace, find pure delight
Capture memories, hold them dear
For time's swift passage is often unclear
Be brave, my love, when darkness falls
Summon courage from deep within your walls
With every stumble, you shall rise
Stronger, wiser, the phoenix flies

The Universe

If you ever need an answer, look to the sky
The universe picks up signals
I can't fully explain why
The energy from your soul pours out into the world
Sending forth your personal needs and emotions
If you truly want something, send out vibes from your heart
Focusing on your needs is a wonderful place to start
Write affirmations towards your goals
You can even meditate and pray
This will help you stay focused throughout your day
Just remember you're not alone
I'll always help you
Even when you're not at home

Transition

The life that was meant for you will always find you —
Just as the swamps run along the coastline,
You can transition during any point of your life.

Two Hearts

In a bond, like no other, they're tied
A mother and a daughter, side by side
With love that's profound,
Their hearts, they have found
In each other's embrace, they confide

Unpaved Roads

Believe in yourself when the going gets tough
Life is full of tests you'll have to overcome
You will come across many unpaved roads and pebbled paths
You can walk around the hardships in life,
Or you can create your own path
Life is about the journey we create and our happiness along the way
Your destination will be waiting for you no matter what
Be sure to enjoy yourself along the way

Validation

My beloved daughter,
Learn that life will become simpler when you stop looking for approval
from others.
The only validation you need is your own.

When you Wake

When you wake, indulge in a morning routine
Brew your favorite coffee beans of caffeine
When you wake, recite positive affirmation and prayers
Take in the silence from your comfortable chairs
When you wake, set daily goals
Make them realistic so you stay in control
When you wake, set the tone to your day
Workout your body before you play
When you wake, journal your dreams
Writing is therapeutic, no matter how odd it may seem
When you wake, be thankful for what you have
Find contentment in the good and the bad
When you wake, you can start anew
The only person holding you back is you

Who You Are

People always say it takes years to find yourself,
But you know exactly who that is.
Embrace who you are to live a fulfilled life.

You are Loved

You are loved
You are cherished
You are perfectly imperfect
I am unbelievably grateful you are my daughter

You Won't Always Need Me

You won't always need me, and that's okay
You are your own person at the end of the day
You won't always need me
You'll be a woman soon enough
You'll know what to do when times get tough
You won't always need me
Your journey is your own
Just remember you are never alone
You won't always need me
In time, you'll walk out the door
There are journeys in life you'll want to explore
You won't always need me,
But I'll need you for the rest of my days

You'll Have a Spot

I'll have a spot just for you
When you're down and feeling blue
You'll have a spot in this house
Through the struggles and the doubts
You'll always have a spot at home
Please know you will never be alone

You'll Make Mistakes

You'll make mistakes throughout your life
This you cannot skip over
At times it will feel like you're dodging knives
This proves you don't always take charge of your controller
You'll make mistakes when choosing friends
And think they'll understand your heart
You'll want acceptance and follow trends
But, in the end, you'll drift apart
Change is good, from time to time
It's how we learn and grow
Know you are truly sublime
Wisdom from experiences throughout your life, you'll bestow
Life is not always what we want
You'll get frustrated in the mess
When flustered, take a break with a buttery croissant
At the end of your path, God knows what is best

You're Growing Up

You're growing up into a beautiful young lady.
I remember when I brought you home from the hospital.
Your tiny toes wiggled with delight when Mommy held you.
Now you're a teenager.
You wear makeup and talk about boys.
I don't know where the time went.
You're growing up, and I see your free spirit from your father.
Your tender heart you get from me.
You never hold your head low when someone attempts to make fun of
you.
You've always known exactly what to say to others.
I'm proud of the girl you are today.
I hope once you're out on your own you still consider my place home.
You are the best part of me.

Young Girl

Young girl, you must break out of your cocoon and transfer into a
butterfly
Change is a part of life, and transformation is an important step in
growth
Young girl, your time to transform must happen when you alone are
ready
You cannot force your path
Young girl, remember that growing your roots is more important than
your image
People will respect you once you've made something of yourself
Young girl, remember to work hard and not be wasteful
If you truly desire something in life,
You must perform constantly to obtain it
Young girl, remember to take breaks along the way so you don't give up

Your Dream

Create your own dream
Live your own life
True happiness comes from accepting that you're allowed to enjoy contentment
If you have to walk down a different path to arrive at your destination,
That's okay

Your Own Path

Walk the path that you create
Carve your stepping stones and build your own gates
The future is undetermined, but it's also bright
Your outcomes are shaped by the chapters you write
Play your music to your own special song
Your heart will never steer you wrong
Dance under the moonlight while others sleep
Do not be offended if people call you the black sheep
As long as your intentions are pure,
The opinions of others should not weigh you down

Don't miss out!

Visit the website below and you can sign up to receive emails whenever Brittany Benko publishes a new book. There's no charge and no obligation.

https://books2read.com/r/B-A-MBYL-JMKUC

BOOKS 2 READ

Connecting independent readers to independent writers.

Also by Brittany Benko

Poetic Poetry: A Short Collection of Poems
Poetic Poems and Prose
The Guiding Pen

Watch for more at https://brittanybenko.wixsite.com/booksbybrittany.

About the Author

Brittany is a self-published poet, Etsy seller, LitPick book reviewer, special needs mother, and law enforcement wife who lives in the Lowcountry of South Carolina. She has been featured in two anthologies: Daydreams and Lost Wishes (A Poetic Reveries Anthology) and South Carolina Bards Anthology 2022. She has been featured as a poet through Spillwords, The Writers Club, The Open-Door Poetry Magazine, the Autism Parenting Magazine, and Poetic Reveries.

Be sure to leave Brittany a review on Goodreads or Bookbub if you enjoyed her book!

Read more at https://brittanybenko.wixsite.com/booksbybrittany.